THE ZACK FILES™

The Volcano Goddess Will See You Now

For Judith, and for the real Zack,
with love—D.G.

THE ZACK FILES™

The Volcano Goddess Will See You Now

By Dan Greenburg

Illustrated by Jack E. Davis

GROSSET & DUNLAP • NEW YORK

I'd like to thank my editors,
Jane O'Connor and Judy Donnelly,
who make the process of writing and revising
so much fun, and without whom
these books would not exist.

I also want to thank
Jennifer Dussling and Laura Driscoll
for their terrific ideas.

Text copyright © 1997 by Dan Greenburg. Illustrations copyright © 1997 by Jack E. Davis. All rights reserved. Published by Grosset & Dunlap, a division of Penguin Young Readers Group, 345 Hudson Street, New York, New York 10014. THE ZACK FILES and GROSSET & DUNLAP are trademarks of Penguin Group (USA) Inc. Printed in the U.S.A.

Library of Congress Cataloging-in-Publication Data
Greenburg, Dan.
    The volcano goddess will see you now / by Dan Greenburg ; illustrated by Jack E. Davis.
        p.   cm. — (The Zack files)
    Summary: Zack and his father go to Hawaii where Zack has an unfortunate encounter with an angry volcano goddess.
    [1. Hawaii—Fiction. 2. Volcanoes—Fiction. 3. Pele (Hawaiian deity)—Fiction.]
I. Davis, Jack E., ill. II. Title. III. Series: Greenburg, Dan. Zack files.
PZ7.G8278Vo 1997
[Fic]—dc21
                                                                        97-16742
                                                                        CIP
ISBN 978-0-448-41559-8   20   19   18   AC

Chapter 1

Most people think of Hawaii as a place to go surfing, eat pineapples, and learn to do the hula dance. Most people wouldn't think of Hawaii as a spooky place where you could fall under the curse of a very grouchy volcano goddess and also skin your knee really badly. Most people would be wrong.

Oh, my name is Zack and I'm ten and a half, in case you were wondering. I live in New York City, half the time with my dad and the other half with my mom. So what was I doing in Hawaii? Well, my dad is a magazine writer. And sometimes he gets sent to really cool places to write about them—for free! This time the really cool place was Hawaii. Dad was writing an article about volcanoes for *Natural Disaster Magazine*. We were even going to get to see a real volcano called Kilauea up close.

It was late at night by the time Dad pulled up in our rental car to the front of the hotel. You couldn't miss it, even in the dark. It was bright pink with about a million palm trees around it. A big neon sign out front said: "Welcome to the Humuhumunukunukuapua'a Hotel!"

"Humu-hamu-noonoo-poopoo...what?" I said.

"Humu-humu-nuku-nuku-apu-ah-ah," Dad said. "It's the name of a Hawaiian fish. Bet you can't say it three times fast."

After Dad finished laughing at his own joke, he pointed to what looked like a small volcano right next to the hotel.

"See that?" he said. "Any second now it's going to erupt."

No sooner had he said this than flames began shooting out of the top.

"Yikes!" I said. "Let's get out of here!"

Dad laughed.

"Don't worry, Zack. It's a fake. After sundown it erupts every hour for the tourists."

Pretty cool. A hot-pink hotel with its very own volcano.

"Well, Zack," said Dad as we dragged our bags into the hotel, "this will be our home for the next week. What do you think?"

I smiled at Dad.

"I think some kids have all the luck," I said.

The inside of the Humuhumunuku-nukuapua'a was almost as cool as the outside. In fact, the inside looked like it *was* the outside. There were millions of palm trees in the lobby. Hanging vines everywhere. And one whole wall was an aquarium. It had fish in all different colors. Also baby sharks. Real baby sharks. I'm not kidding. They weren't cute or anything, though. They looked just like the shark in *Jaws*, except they were only about a foot long.

We walked to the elevators.

"Aloha!" a hotel lady in a grass skirt greeted us.

"Aloha!" Dad and I answered her. You're supposed to do that anytime anybody says aloha to you or they'll think you're rude.

"Welcome to Hawaii," she said.

She put necklaces made of little orchids

around our necks. I think they're called leis. Mine smelled pretty good, but I felt goofy wearing it.

We were just about to press the elevator button when I heard a blood-curdling scream. I jumped about six inches off the ground.

"What the heck was that?" I asked.

"Look over there," said the hotel lady. She was laughing.

Off to our right was this huge red and blue parrot. It let out another screech and looked at me, like it was getting a big kick out of scaring me out of my shorts. This parrot was standing on a perch, right out in the open. I guess they weren't too worried about parrot poop on their carpet.

"We call her Pele, after the Hawaiian volcano goddess," the hotel lady told us.

"Pele wanna cracker?" I joked.

The parrot rolled an eye at me.

"Pele wanna bite your butt!" it shrieked.

"Oh, don't mind her," the hotel lady said, taking my arm. "She has a nasty temper. Just like the goddess."

Dad pressed the elevator button.

"Do people really believe there's a volcano goddess?" I asked her.

"You bet," she said. "We take our goddesses very seriously around here. It's not smart to get Pele mad at you."

"Well, we'll be sure to stay on her good side," I said.

I didn't know how seriously to take this volcano goddess business. I wasn't ready to laugh it off, though. Not too long ago I had a pretty weird encounter with an Egyptian cat goddess named Bast. But that's a whole other story.

Just then the elevator doors swished open. A minute later Dad and I were in our room. Only it wasn't just a room.

It was the Humuhumunukunukuapua'a Hibiscus Suite. I flopped down on one of the two giant water beds.

"Dad," I said, "this place is huge. It's practically the size of your whole apartment! Did we luck out or what?"

Dad turned on one of the floor lamps. The base of it was in the shape of a hula dancer. I checked out all the cool stuff in the suite. Our TV was almost as big as a movie screen. There was a mini-bar full of all my favorite candy bars, and the bathroom had a shell-shaped tub with a Jacuzzi in it.

Dad opened the sliding glass doors and we went out on the terrace. Our suite looked right out over the beach and the pool, which was squiggly-shaped like a real lagoon. The pool had all kinds of waterfalls and stuff.

"Just think, Zack," said Dad. "Tomorrow we'll be catching rays and riding waves."

I nodded. It was going to be great. More than great, in fact. But right now I was pretty sleepy. We'd been on the plane for around a hundred hours.

"You know," said Dad as I climbed into my water bed, "I have a feeling this is one trip we're never going to forget."

Well, Dad was sure right about that. But not in the way he meant.

Chapter 2

"Dad! Wake up!" I yelled.

It was kind of early the next morning. Dad didn't answer, so I threw open the curtains and bounced down next to him on his water bed. A wave rolled across the bed and jolted him awake.

"Hey!" Dad grumbled.

"Come on, Dad. Wake up! I've already had breakfast down in the dining room," I said. "I had a pineapple muffin, a ham and pineapple omelette, and a glass of cran-pineapple juice. They sure seem to like pineapples over here."

"Mmmmph," said Dad sleepily.

"Well, I'm ready for the beach," I said. "What about you?"

Dad sat up and rubbed his eyes.

"OK, OK," he said. "Just give me a minute."

He gave me a quick look. I already had my swim trunks on.

"Did you remember to put on lots of sunscreen?" he asked.

Oops. I knew I was forgetting something. I looked all over but I didn't see my sunscreen anywhere. It was a brand-new bottle that Dad had bought just for the trip. I couldn't think where I'd left it. And then I could.

"I just remembered where I left the sunscreen," I said.

"Where?"

"On the sink in the bathroom."

"Well then, go in there and get it."

"On the sink in the bathroom in New York," I said.

Dad sighed. "OK. Go down to the gift shop, buy some sunscreen, and charge it to the room."

So off I went. The lobby was kind of empty. Probably because it was seven A.M.

The gift shop was empty, too. It took me no time to find a tube of sunscreen, and I went up to the counter to pay.

Next to the cash register was a basket of little souvenirs for sale. Little tiki dolls. Pineapple keychains. I happen to love souvenirs, but I couldn't decide what to buy. Then I saw a piece of lava for only a quarter. Cool!

I charged the sunscreen and the lava and I left.

On my way back to our suite I took a closer look at my piece of lava. It was dull and black, and it had little holes all over it. The lava was glued to a piece of cardboard. On the cardboard it said: "This lava is definitely *not* from Kilauea Volcano."

I didn't know why it said that. So what if it wasn't from Kilauea? I didn't care. It was still cool. I stuck it in my pocket and forgot all about it.

Dad had better be awake and ready, I thought. If not I was going to bounce on his bed so hard I'd create a tidal wave.

Chapter 3

You'll never guess what color the sand on the beach was. Black!

"What's wrong with the sand?" I asked Dad. "Is it dirty or what?"

"No, no," he said. "It's black because it's ground-up lava. From Kilauea." Then he pointed to a huge volcano in the distance. "There she is," he said. "Kilauea. Tomorrow we'll take a ride up there and say hello to her in person."

That was fine with me. But right now all I wanted was to go swimming. So I smeared on some sunscreen and headed for the water.

"Not so fast, Zack!" Dad called. He had his camera out and was waving to one of the cabana guys who bring you towels and stuff when you're on the beach.

"Could you take a picture of us with the volcano in the background?" Dad asked him.

The cabana guy had us stand right by this giant palm tree. He put a lei around my neck. "Now you look like a real Hawaiian," he said. Then he peered through the camera. "Smile and say Waikiki!"

Dad and I smiled and said Waikiki. The cabana guy snapped the picture and I suddenly saw stars. Lots of them. Which was weird, because no flashbulb had gone off or anything. The next thing I knew I was lying facedown in the sand.

Dad was leaning over me.

"Zack, are you all right?" he kept asking.

"Pretty much," I said, sitting up. "What happened?"

"This," he said.

Dad was holding a coconut. "It fell from the palm tree and hit you on the head."

"Wow!" said the cabana guy, shaking his head. "What are the chances of *that* happening? I've worked here five years and I've never seen anybody get clonked like that."

"I guess I'm just lucky," I mumbled. I dusted black sand off my body. Dad looked at my head.

"You're OK," he said. "But in an hour or so you are going to have quite a bump. Why don't I take you back up to the suite. You can keep the coconut as a souvenir."

"Ha, ha," I said.

I wanted to stay right here on the beach. I hadn't even made it into the water yet. But

Dad's mind was made up. So we went back to our suite. And while he worked on his magazine story out on the terrace, I lay down on my water bed and watched TV. Somehow this wasn't what I imagined doing on my first morning in Hawaii.

There was a program on about ghosts in Hawaii. I didn't realize they had ghosts in Hawaii. Somehow you think of ghosts being in cold, drafty old houses. Not in hot, sunny places with beaches and palm trees.

After a while the picture on the TV got kind of fuzzy. So fuzzy, in fact, I could hardly see the program. And the sound got really buzzy. Had I gotten bonked on the head harder than I thought? I started to get up to change the channel. That's when I heard it. This very strange voice coming from the TV. **"You...have...something...that... belongs...to...me!"** was what it said.

It really gave me the creeps. I couldn't

tell if it was from the program about ghosts or if it was coming from another channel.

"Dad..." I called out.

"You...have...something...that... belongs...to...me!"

Dad couldn't hear me through the sliding glass door. I decided to turn off the TV. That's when it decided to explode.

Dad ran in from the terrace. Little pieces of glass from the TV had been blasted everywhere. Luckily none of them had hit me, but our hula-girl floor lamp got beheaded. And Dad's water bed had sprung a leak.

The hotel manager was very sorry about the TV and about our suite. He promised to move us to another room. He also gave us free passes to the spa. So Dad and I went downstairs to the spa while the hotel guys moved all our stuff to the new room.

At the spa we got fluffy white bathrobes

and free bottles of pineapple juice. Dad went to the weight area to work out with dumbbells. I headed for the treadmills.

I've always liked treadmills. I'm not sure why. You stand on this moving belt and you run in place. It's sort of fun, except when you realize you're running really hard and not going anywhere. But that's what tread-mills are for. Going nowhere fast.

I took off my robe and got on. I don't like to brag. But I happen to be the third best runner in the fifth grade at the Horace Hyde-White School for Boys. Dad had warned me not to go too fast on the treadmill, since I'd just gotten clonked on the head by a coconut. So I set the speed for five miles per hour.

I started jogging. 3.5 miles per hour... 4.0...4.2.... The digital numbers got higher. Soon I was trotting along just fine at five miles per hour. But then something really weird happened. The treadmill kept speeding up. 5.5...6.0...6.7.... I pushed the button to make it slow down, but it didn't work. I wasn't jogging anymore. I was running! 7.3...7.5...7.9.... What was going on here?

"Excuse me, sir!" I shouted to one of the spa guys. "I think something is wrong with this machine!"

Nobody heard me.

8.3...8.6...8.9.... I was really moving now! I pushed the stop button. Nothing. I pushed every button in sight, but it didn't do any good.

"Excuse me! This machine is going berserk!" I yelled.

That's when it threw me off, just like a bucking bronco. Right onto the floor. I landed on my butt. Hard. I also skinned my knee.

Dad saw me go flying, and he came running over.

"Zack, are you all right?" he asked.

"I guess so," I said. "I don't know what happened. It was so weird. The machine went nuts!"

"Zack, I think maybe a doctor should take a look at you," said Dad. "Let's go back up to the room."

"Dad, come on. There's nothing wrong with me," I said. I was here in Hawaii to have fun. But then I stood up. I did feel a little woozy. Maybe Dad was right. Maybe I *did* need to see a doctor.

Dad put in a call to the hotel doctor. He made an appointment for the doctor to meet us back at our new room. As we left the spa, I overheard two of the spa guys talking.

"I've never seen that happen before," said one of them. "Somebody getting thrown off the treadmill like that."

"Me neither," said the other guy. "Not in the eight years I've worked here."

Funny. That was almost the same thing the cabana guy said when I got conked on the head by the coconut.

We went up to our new room. It wasn't a suite this time. Just a room. But it had a TV and a mini-bar and it was still pretty nice. There wasn't a view of the pool from our terrace. But if you leaned way out you could kind of see the fake volcano.

"You sure seem to be having a run of bad luck today," said Dad. "First the coconut bonks you on the head. Then the TV explodes. And now you go flying off the treadmill."

"Yeah," I said. "I hope there won't be anything else."

"I don't think there will be," said Dad. "I've heard these things come in threes."

"I hope you're right," I said.

That's when the mini-bar in our new room burst into flames.

Chapter 4

How we handled the flaming mini-bar was we raced out into the hall and screamed. Then Dad spotted a fire extinguisher in a glass case in the hallway. He broke the glass and got it out. Then he went back into our room and started spraying foam all over the place. Finally he put out the fire.

Now our new room was as big a mess as the old one. There was foam everywhere. It looked like the room had been hit by a major snowstorm. That's when the hotel doctor appeared in the doorway.

"What's going on here?" she asked.

"Our mini-bar burst into flames," Dad told her.

"I thought I was supposed to check on someone who fell off a treadmill."

"Right. That was me, too," I said. "I sort of banged my butt and skinned my knee when I landed on the floor. I also have a bump on my head. But not from the treadmill. I got hit by a falling coconut this morning."

"You folks are having some kind of day," she said. She started examining me.

"Just a little bad luck," said Dad. "It happens."

"Falling off a treadmill is a little bad luck," said the doctor. "Getting clunked on the head and having your mini-bar burst into flames puts you in a whole new category."

"Oh, did I mention our TV exploded?" I said.

The doctor laughed and shook her head.

"Hey, you haven't gotten old Madame Pele mad at you, now have you?" she said.

"Madame Pele?" I said. "You mean the volcano goddess?"

The doctor nodded.

"I was just reading up on her," said Dad. "For the magazine article I'm writing."

"The ancient Hawaiians believed Madame Pele lived inside Kilauea," said the doctor. "The volcano erupted every time she got angry. And she got angry very easily. So they kept her happy with sacrifices of pigs...and young boys," she added, looking at me.

"Get out of here," I said.

"I'm serious," she said. "And there are many people today who believe Madame Pele is just as angry and powerful as she ever was."

I didn't like hearing what the doctor had

said. Madame Pele sounded as if she were the kind of goddess who wouldn't mind turning someone's dream vacation into a nightmare. But why would such a thing be happening to me? I'd just gotten here. What could I have done to make her so mad at me?

No sooner had the doctor left than the hotel manager arrived to inspect the damage to our second room. Once again he was very sorry, and he promised to move us to a new room right away. Unfortunately, the only room they had left was a very small one, and it didn't even have a mini-bar.

This vacation was definitely not turning out the way I'd planned. But why? That was the big question. I mean why was I having such a run of bad luck?

I always think better on a full stomach, so I headed to the lobby to buy some candy. At the hotel newsstand I loaded up on

M&M's and Snickers. As I was leaving I noticed a metal rack filled with the kind of newspapers you always see in supermarket checkout lines. The ones with stories about little gray aliens from outer space. And two-headed babies. And people who have cats as big as ponies. One headline caught my eye right away:

REVENGE OF THE VOLCANO GODDESS

ROTTEN LUCK FOR LAVA LOVERS!

Aha!

Maybe this newspaper could tell me what was happening to me. I bought the paper and began to read. Something very strange was definitely going on in Hawaii. And I was determined to get to the bottom of it.

Chapter 5

"Dad! Wait till you hear this!" I yelled as I burst into the room.

Dad was by the window, checking out the view of the hotel parking lot. I went over and shook the newspaper in his face.

"Look! I found out what's been causing all my bad luck," I shouted. "It makes perfect sense. I'm under a curse!"

Dad pushed the newspaper away. "A curse? Hey, c'mon, Zack," he said. "I know it's been a rough day. But a streak of bad luck does not mean you're under any curse."

"No, listen to me," I said. "This newspaper story explained it perfectly."

"Where did you get that thing?"

"I bought it downstairs. Just look at this headline."

Dad looked at the newspaper. "You mean this one? 'ELVIS WAS AN ALIEN! FAKED OWN DEATH AND RETURNED TO MOTHER SHIP!'"

"No, no, this one about volcanoes." I pointed to the article.

"Zack," said Dad, "you really can't believe what you read in these tabloids. They make most of it up."

"Maybe so," I said. "But not this. Just let me read you a little bit of the article, OK?"

Dad sighed and sat down on the bed. "Go ahead," he said.

So I sat down next to him and started to read: "'A woman's hair sucked off in a freak vacuuming accident. A man's Volkswagen Beetle crushed by a two-ton meteor, leaving only the tailpipe intact. A kid's teddy bear shredded in a squirrel attack.

"'What do these people have in common? All three had recently visited Hawaii and taken lava from Kilauea Volcano as a souvenir. Hawaiian legend says that Pele, the jealous and vengeful volcano goddess of Kilauea, puts a curse on all her lava. Every year, lava-loving tourists report strange incidents of bad luck. Most end up sending back their lava, begging park rangers to return it directly to Madame Pele. They ask the park rangers to plead for Madame Pele's forgiveness.

"'Many native Hawaiians believe that throwing stolen lava back into the volcano at night is the only way to break the curse. Others say this is superstitious nonsense.

"'So, is there really a curse? Or is it

just bad luck? Just coincidence? You decide!'"

I looked up at Dad. "Well," I said. "What do you think now?"

"It's interesting, Zack," he said. "But what does it have to do with you? You haven't even been to Kilauea yet. And you certainly don't have any lava."

I cleared my throat. "Actually, Dad..." I reached into my pocket and pulled out the piece of lava. "I bought this in the gift shop this morning."

"Hmmmmm," was all Dad said. He was reading the label on the cardboard.

"Dad," I went on, "what if all my accidents weren't just accidents? What if this lava really *is* from Kilauea? What if Madame Pele is good and mad at me? What if she's put a curse on me?"

"Zack," said Dad, "I really don't think that's what's going on here. But we're going to Kilauea anyway tomorrow. Just throw your piece of lava into the volcano and see what happens."

"Dad," I said, "the newspaper story says the only way to break the curse is to throw it back at *night*."

"Day, night..." Dad shrugged. "I doubt that it makes any diff—"

Ker-WHAM! The bed we were sitting on crashed to the floor. Dad looked at me.

"On second thought," he said, "it might be a good idea to go right now."

Chapter 6

Kilauea loomed ahead of us. Its chimney was a thousand feet high. Its crater was almost three miles across. A steady column of orange smoke and steam was billowing out of the crater. It was a pretty scary sight.

The road to the crater snaked upward through the woods. For the last part of the way, the road was so narrow, we had to get out of the car and walk. The wind was blowing so hard it sounded like it was whining. Whining wind doesn't usually bother me all that much. But tonight it did. Then I thought I heard something else. A creepy voice in the wind.

"Dad, do you hear anything?" I asked.

"Just the wind," he said.

The wind kept whining. And above it I could now definitely make out this really creepy voice: **"You...have...something...that...belongs...to...me!"**

"There, did you hear that?" I asked. "That really creepy voice?"

"Zack," said Dad, "how could you be hearing creepy voices? There's nobody out here but us."

"Are you sure?"

"Pretty sure," he said.

"*Pretty* sure? You mean you're not positive?"

We both started walking faster.

The voice came again: **"You...have...something...that...belongs...to...me! Give...it...back!"**

"That's why we came!" I yelled at the wind. "Just hold your horses!"

We got to the rim of the crater. I peeked over the edge. A thousand feet below me was something that looked like orange porridge. Very, very hot orange porridge. Dad told me that molten lava is ten times as hot as boiling water. And if you fall into a volcano, you vaporize. That means you turn into steam. Which would really limit the types of things you could do on a vacation.

I took out my lava rock.

"All right, Madame Pele," I yelled. "Here's your darn rock back! Now leave us alone, OK?" Then I threw it as hard as I could right into the volcano.

"There," I said to Dad. "Pele should be happy now."

"I guess we'll find out," Dad answered. "C'mon, Zack. If we hurry we can get back in time for the luau tonight."

Chapter 7

"Now *this* is what I call a vacation," I said to Dad. "A luau by the pool."

I sat back, took a sip of my Pineapple Paradise drink, and twirled the little pink paper umbrella in my glass.

I was feeling pretty happy. It had been almost an hour since we left the volcano, and nothing bad had happened. I mean nothing. Nothing shattered. Nothing fell on my head. Nothing exploded. Nothing burst into flames. It was almost dull.

This luau, on the other hand, was definitely going to be exciting, in a normal, no-curse, no-mad-goddess kind of way. Dad and I had the best table in the place. It was right next to the big waterfall by the pool, so we'd have a perfect view of the Lagoonies. They were the Humuhumunukunuku-apua'a's very own swimming hula dancers.

"Zack." Dad nudged me in the ribs. "Look what's coming our way."

I looked behind me. A parade of waiters carrying all kind of fancy trays and stuff stopped in front of our table. Two guys with giant flaming tiki torches stood on either side of Dad and me as the waiters served our dinner.

There was some kind of brown gunk called poi. There was a whole roast pig with an apple stuck in its mouth. There was a tray full of little appetizers that was called a puupuu platter. I swear I'm not making that up!

I had just started eating my puupuu, poi, and roast pig when I heard this really loud drumroll. A voice boomed out of a loudspeaker. "And now...ladies and gentlemen...the moment you've all been waiting for...Humuhumunukunuku apua'a's very own water ballerinas...the Lagoonies!"

Suddenly these bright green, blue, and pink spotlights shone down on twenty women standing in a row by the side of the pool. They were each wearing weird pineapple headdresses and swimsuits with these little grass skirts made of plastic. One by one, they dove sideways into the pool and began a hula dance in the water.

I had never seen anything like it.

I leaned back in my chair and took another sip of Pineapple Paradise. It was a beautiful, warm starry night. And here I was in Hawaii. Back home, the kids I knew were freezing their buns off. I sure was one lucky kid.

Then I had to laugh. It was the first time all day I'd thought I was lucky. I turned to Dad.

"Boy, am I glad I got rid of that lava," I said.

I'd barely finished that sentence when all of a sudden I heard this really loud sound behind me. PFFSST! It was like when you shake up a bottle of soda and it spurts out all over the place. Only about a million times louder.

"Look out!" someone shouted. "The waterfall!"

I was just turning around to see, when a tidal wave of water hit Dad and me so hard it sent us flying into the pool!

We landed with a splash, right in the middle of the Lagoonies. My leg got tangled underwater in one Lagoonie's grass skirt. Then another Lagoonie accidentally knocked me in the face with her pineapple headdress.

Finally, sputtering and coughing, I made it up for air. All the hotel guests were applauding. I guess they thought Dad and I were part of the act.

"What a great end to the show!" somebody said.

"Wait, it's not over yet," said somebody else. "Look at the volcano!"

Dad and I paddled to the edge of the pool and looked up. Smoke was pouring out the top of the fake volcano. But the weird thing was the smoke seemed to be forming letters. First a G. Then an I. Then a V. Soon a bunch of words were spelled out in curly smoking letters across the sky:

GIVE IT BACK, ZACK!

What? Not Pele again!

Dad and I scrambled out of the pool.

"Dad, I gave Pele back her darn lava!" I shouted. "I don't understand why I'm still under a curse!"

Dad turned to me. We were both dripping wet.

"I don't either," he said. "And what's more, I don't care! You go up to the room to pack. I'm going to the front desk. I'm booking us on the next plane out of here!"

That was fine with me. I'd had enough of Hawaii. I went back to our room. Wherever I walked I left a river of water. As soon as I got back to the room, I changed into dry clothes and started packing. Well, I thought bitterly, at least I got in one swim before I left. Too bad I didn't get to eat at the luau. I was starving. I called room service and ordered a cheeseburger and fries.

I was busy stuffing underwear into my duffel bag when I heard somebody knocking at the door. It wasn't knocking exactly. It was more like pounding. I figured maybe it was room service. I went to the door and opened it.

Standing in the doorway was something dreadful. A terrible looking old lady with wild red hair and crazy red eyes. She was about seven feet tall. She was also on fire, but that didn't seem to bother her. I was pretty sure she wasn't from room service.

Chapter 8

The terrible on-fire old lady stared at me with her crazy red eyes. The flames made a kind of low, crackling roar behind her.

"You...have...something...that... belongs...to...me!" she said. Only she didn't say it. She kind of thundered and lightninged it.

I was so scared I couldn't move. Or speak.

"You...have...something...that... belongs...to...me!" she thundered again.

"N-no, I d-don't," I croaked. "I threw it b-back in the volcano tonight."

"You...have...something...that...belongs...to...me!" she shouted again, only louder.

As scared as I was, I can't stand it when somebody accuses me unfairly. Or repeats herself.

"Hey, give me a break," I said. "I don't have it anymore."

"'Hey, give me a break?'" she shrieked. **"This is how you speak to a volcano goddess? This is how you were taught? 'Hey, give me a break?'"**

She seemed really mad.

"Hey, give me a break, your highness," I said. "I threw the lava back into your volcano—I swear. Didn't you see it or what?"

"No!" she roared.

Her voice was so loud, it rattled the sliding glass door to the balcony.

"Well, could your highness maybe go back and look a little harder?" I suggested.

She walked into the room. Well, not walked exactly. It was more like floating. The drapes on the sliding glass door caught fire. She blew them out, like you'd blow out a birthday candle.

"You still have something that belongs to me!" she roared again.

This time the sliding glass door had had it. Little spiderwebby cracks spread across it. Then it collapsed on the floor in a shower of tiny pieces.

"So what you're saying is I have something *else* that belongs to you?" I asked. "Is that it, your highness?"

"Yes!"

"But I bought only one piece of lava in the gift shop," I said. "What else of yours could I possibly have? Is it something besides lava, your highness?"

"Something *besides* lava?" she thundered. "How could it be something *besides* lava? You think maybe I loaned you a sweater?"

"No, no, of course not, your highness," I said. "OK, so it's another piece of lava. I don't know how I could have gotten another piece of lava, but I believe you. Now where could it be?"

As Madame Pele roared and crackled at the door, I began to search the room. I looked in my suitcase. I looked in the closet. I looked in all of my dresser drawers.

"Did you check the nightstand?"

"Uh, no. Thanks," I said. "I'll do that."

I checked the nightstand. There wasn't any lava in it.

"Did you check your father's suitcase?"

"Uh, no. Thanks. I'll do that too."

I checked my dad's suitcase. There wasn't any lava there either.

"Did you check the pockets of your jeans?" she thundered.

"What jeans?"

"The ones in the closet?"

"Oh, no. Thanks. I'll check that too."

I went to the closet and checked the pockets of my jeans. I didn't think there'd be any lava in them. There wasn't.

"Do you know what a mess this closet is?"

I looked at the closet. It really was kind of sloppy. A lot of my stuff wasn't hung up properly. Shirts and stuff were jammed in at odd angles. There were dirty clothes all over the floor.

"I'm sorry, your highness," I said. "I need to straighten up in there, I guess."

"You can say that again!"

Just then the waiter from room service

arrived with a covered metal tray. The door was open, so he knocked on the doorway.

"Come in," I said.

He came into the room. He saw the seven-foot flaming Madame Pele. His eyes got very wide. He dropped the tray and ran. I picked up the food and put it back on the tray.

"What is that?" she demanded.

"Just something I ordered from room service, your highness," I said. "A cheeseburger and fries."

"A cheesburger and fries? This is a meal for a growing boy?"

"Well, that's about what they have," I said. "Why, what do you eat, your highness?"

"What do I eat?" she shrieked. **"I eat growing boys, that's what I eat!"**

I backed away from her.

"I'm kidding, I'm kidding," she said.

"What's the matter, can't you take a joke? Eating boys was in the olden days. Human sacrifice was big then. Everybody did it. What did we know? Nowadays I eat mainly salads and low-fat yogurt. Take off your shoes."

"Excuse me?"

"I said take off your shoes!"

I took off my sneakers.

"Shake them out!"

I did. In the toe of my right one was a tiny piece of gravel.

"See? There it is!"

I looked at the piece of gravel.

"Holy cow!" I said. "It's actually a tiny piece of lava!"

"What did I tell you!"

I held it out to her. She reached for it with flaming fingers. They nearly singed my skin.

"It must have gotten into my sneaker by

mistake," I said. "I'm sorry, your highness. I didn't take it on purpose. I really
didn't. I swear."

"All right, all right," she said. **"I heard
you. Be quiet."**

"I'm really sorry to have taken that from
you," I said.

**"Well, I'm sorry to have caused such
a fuss. All right, I guess I'll be going."**

"OK," I said. "Well, nice meeting you."

"You too, kid," she said. **"So when are
you flying back to the mainland?"**

"We were going to leave tonight," I said.
"But I guess maybe now we'll stay for a few
days."

"Well, enjoy the rest of your trip."

"Thanks," I said. "I'll try to."

**"When you go to the pool, be sure to
wear sunblock. At least SPF 15. Other-
wise you could get a nasty burn. Or
even sunstroke, God forbid."**

"OK," I said. "Thanks for the tip."

"You seem like a nice boy."

"Thanks," I said. "You seem like a nice volcano goddess."

"How many of them have you met?"

"Not that many."

"Then that's not much of a compliment, is it?"

"Sorry."

"Well, I have to be getting back to the crater. Don't take any more of my lava or you'll regret it. I'm not as nice as I seem. You just caught me on a good day."

There was a sudden flash of blinding light. And then she was gone.

Chapter 9

Dad and I ended up staying for the week. The hotel was pretty understanding about our room, for the most part. I don't know if they bought the story about Madame Pele's visit, though. They did make us pay for a new sliding glass door and new drapes. Dad is going to try and put it on his expense account from the magazine.

On Saturday Dad and I went to the airport. A wrinkly old man came up to me. His face looked like leather gloves that had been out in the rain and left on a radiator to dry. He had flowered leis around his neck. He was carrying all kinds of junk to sell to tourists.

"Souvenirs of Hawaii," he said. "You wish?"

"Not really," I said. "Unless you have any baseball cards?"

"No, no," he said. "No baseball cards. But I have something better."

He held it out to me.

"What's that?"

"Souvenirs of Hawaii," he said. "Pieces of lava. Guaranteed not to be from Kilauea."

I screamed and ran.

What else happens to Zack?
Find out in

Bozo the Clone

Now the hand was followed by an arm. Then a second hand slid out of the box. The hands pushed back the lid of the box. And out climbed...me! I mean it was a perfect copy of the way I looked in my school picture. The same sticking-up hair, the same goofy grin...

Yikes! I'd created Bozo the clone!